Erotic Short Stories for Women

Dirty Group Sex

Rough Erotica Short Stories

Vivienne Dupont

Table of Contents

Birthday Sex in Swingers Club

It was the 15th of July. It was a terrible day. I'd never liked this day. I'd never been eager to celebrate this day. But I had never been able to get around it. This day was the day I was born. Not that I regretted coming into the world or anything. On the contrary really, otherwise I would never have met my friend Robin and that would have been a disaster. But more that, I've never been much of a party person. I couldn't hold my liquor anyway, and being the centre of attention wasn't for me either. But today, I couldn't seem to get away with it.

My two best friends Susan and Melina, wanted to organise a party for me. But they'd promised me that it would be nothing *big.*

Robin had to go to a meeting and I was bored to death in his penthouse. By now it was five o'clock in the afternoon when I reached for my cell phone and scrolled soullessly through several birthday wishes. Then I heard the apartment door open and I looked up. Susan walked in with two large paper bags in hand and someone in tow. It was a young woman with wide hips, large breasts and a narrow waist. She had long straight golden blonde hair and large green eyes. Her lips were thin, but her grin was wide. They both wore everyday clothes. I raised my eyebrows and sat down on the sofa.

"Hey Mia. We were able to get off work early today. Melina is organising the rest of the party. Meet my colleague and good friend from accounting. This is Hayden Stewart. She's coming to the party. Her father works as an editor at the New Yorker," she introduced Hayden to me and I gave her a friendly nod.

"So you're Mia...", Hayden eyed me slightly suspiciously, but then grinned widely again.

"Yeah. That's me. You sound so... Amazed...?"

"Well, you are something of a minor celebrity," Hayden said directly, sitting down next to me on the sofa. She propped her arm up and scanned me from top to bottom.

"I'm not an animal at the zoo that you can just look at. So please don't do that," I said to her and rolled my eyes.

"You'll have to excuse Hayden. She's naturally curious and the subject of ROMI is the number one topic of conversation behind closed doors," Susan whispered and Hayden nodded eagerly.

"ROMI? What is that supposed to be?", I was almost speechless.

"ROMI. A composite of your names. Mia and Robin. Romi. Cute, right? And so romantic," Hayden sighed and I nearly vomited.

"Oh, my God, you guys are really out of your minds." I laughed.

“Your father is an editor at the New Yorker, right? I'm impressed," I said curiously, trying to change the subject.

"Yes. Why, are you interested?"

"I studied journalism and my dream would be to work at a hip newspaper or magazine as an assistant."

"I could ask my father if they're looking for employees. I'll let you know then. Now can we get to the really important topic of the evening?" asked Hayden jitterily and I guessed what was coming.

"Yeah right, that's actually why we came up here. What are you wearing tonight?", Susan asked me, waving the paper bags.

"I was thinking of a light blue evening gown," I said, shrugging my shoulders.

"Evening gown? You're not going to the opera?! ", Hayden spoke in dismay and widened her eyes.

Then Susan dumped the contents of both bags out on the huge couch and I glanced around among quite a few articles of clothing. Colourful. Brightly colored. Long and short. Very short. Some things looked like a scrap of fabric. I held up what looked like a fishing net. Perforated and I wondered greatly how you couldn't see through this. Bra and panties would definitely be visible. Probably that was the way it was meant to be. I was just about to let it disappear inconspicuously into one of the bags when Hayden quickly grabbed it.

"Oh there it is, I've been looking for that! Isn't it great?" she said joyfully and held it in front of her torso.

"Um... I don't know... What's that supposed to be?", I asked, biting my lips.

"You can tell, it's a minidress," she said indignantly and I had to stifle a laugh. Susan also snorted and looked at the piece of fabric.

"Well, it's pretty daring. You're not going to wear that to the party, are you? It might send the wrong signals," I said, shaking my head.

"I'd put something under it, too!" said Hayden, rolling her eyes.

"Oh really what? I thought that's all you were wearing! ", now I could not hold back the laughter and I almost came to tears.

I had a feeling Hayden would probably find me as strange as I found her. But it didn't matter. She was delightfully refreshing.

"Can we get ready here at your place? Then we could all go to the party together. Or do you think Mr. Robin would mind?", Susan asked me and she looked around in awe.

I still found it amusing that my boyfriend made such an impression on my friends. But well, he was the owner of a large software company for which some of my friends worked. Swann Holding AG had a worldwide presence and I had been looking for a simple office job a few months ago, since I couldn't get a job anywhere at a magazine or publishing house of my choice. And so one thing quickly led to another. I fell in love with Robin Swann and he fell in love with me. Hard to believe, but true. It was kind of a Cinderella story. I had recently started living with him in his penthouse, which was on the top floor of his corporate building. Personally, it wouldn't bother me to never really be able to separate work and private life, but Robin was different.

"No, I don't think so. And since today is my... Birthday... he's very relaxed with everything anyway. He'll catch up anyway, since he's still in a meeting, which I'm sure will take longer again. So it's all good.

So where's the party going to be?", I asked curiously and went to the kitchen on the opposite side to get myself something to drink.

"Not in an opera. That's for sure," Hayden winked at me and she started to undress.

I was amazed when several tattoos appeared. Many colourful flowers and stars were on her thigh, stomach and along the back. She looked like a little painting. She was definitely sexy. Extremely so, in fact. I swallowed hard as I looked at her.

"And not in a restaurant, either," Susan replied, and she, too, disrobed.

"That sounds promising. Except that doesn't leave a lot of options. I hate surprises. You know that, or at least you do Susan," I said.

"You'll love it, I'm sure. Can I use the bathroom?", Hayden asked, clomping around the room dressed only in her bra and thong.

"Please, help yourself," I said, slightly annoyed, and lay lengthwise on the couch.

When Hayden had gone into the bathroom, Susan pressed herself against me on the couch. We used to have something together, but that was actually long gone. She ran her fingers along my breasts and kissed my neck.

I tingled slightly and bit my lips, "Susan... What are you doing? I'm taken with Robin and I'm very happy," I heaved a sigh.

"I know. But I also know you're bi and love men as well as women. That's why your birthday present suits you so well," Susan breathed and played with my nipples.

"What is it, then? Come on, tell me!" I urged her energetically, quivering under her touch.

"Alright. I'll tell you, but don't tell Hayden I told you. We're... We're going to a swingers club. To the new club *Tabulos,*" Susan whispered in my ear, then nibbled on it again.

"That sounds exciting. Best not tell Robin about it. He'll probably have to work late anyway." I gestured.

"Let's go see what Hayden's up to. She's a little crazy, but she's a good soul, at least I think so," I said and took her hand and we walked towards the bathroom together.

When Susan and I entered the bathroom, we were greeted by a tangy heavy scent and copious amounts of hairspray hung in the air. Hayden was in her rag of fabric and wearing endlessly high stilettos. She had her long blonde hair perfectly curled and her green eyes were rimmed with thick kohl. She looked like a work of art, a little cheap, but that was always in the eye of the beholder.

"Hayden... Are you serious? I want Mia to be the centre of attention tonight, not you! " Susan crossed her arms in front of her chest.

"No, no. I'm happy to let her go first." I rebuffed, shaking my head decisively, and walked out of the bathroom and to the closet or wardrobe.

I let my gaze drag over my wardrobe and then called out as if I knew nothing, "So where are we going, anyway?"

"Actually, this was supposed to be a secret," Susan said, playfully contrite, coming over to me.

"Then shut up too," Hayden said, strutting up and down the dressing room.

"I'd like to know where we're going though, so I know what to wear?", I was annoyed.

"I'd go to the opera in this outfit, too," Hayden said, surveying herself from top to bottom. I'd like to have Hayden's confidence. She really made you feel like she wasn't arriving somewhere, she was appearing. Kind of cool!

"How about this dress? It's elegant but doesn't quite look opera yet" Susan asked, taking a knee length silver strappy dress off the rack. I nodded affirmatively, because I didn't want to look too cheap now either. Even though I was already very excited inside.

Susan opted for a blue long halter dress which made her breasts look even bigger. After another hour we were done. Susan and Hayden had curled my hair until it fell down my back in perfect waves. I didn't use more than mascara and eyeliner. When Susan's cell phone vibrated, she grabbed her purse, Hayden did the same.

"Cedric is here. He's taking us to the party. For your information Mia, Cedric is my boyfriend," Hayden winked at me and we walked out of the penthouse and to the elevator.

Cedric had parked right behind the building. Susan, Hayden, and I arrived at the car, which was blasting loud techno. Cedric was driving a dark blue Audi. Very fancy. I went to open the passenger door, but someone was already sitting there. And that someone was Julian. Julian was my ex-boyfriend. More or less. We'd been seeing each other a few times. There was definitely love involved with him, but not with me.

I rolled my eyes and stared at Susan, who was about to open the door in the back.

"What's he doing here?"

"Julian and Cedric have been good friends for quite some time. Does it bother you?" asked Susan, shrugging her shoulders.

"I think it's awesome that Julian's in. He's so fucking hot. Maybe I'll give him a try tonight. Or do you possibly mind Mia?", Hayden grinned and adjusted her scrap of fabric.

"Me? Not in the least. He's yours," I said, bored.

"Ladies, are we going to do anything today?" shouted Cedric, sticking his head out the driver's window.

We slid, I of course a little awkward, on the back seat and then drove crisscross through San Francisco. My ears were ringing from the loud music, but at least I didn't have to talk to Julian. His confession of love was still on my mind more than once. It was dark and I didn't even recognize the area around me anymore. Then, after what felt like an eternity, we stopped in front of a large house, which stood quite apart from a quiet main street. It looked very modern to me and at the entrance a doorman greeted us and held the door open for us.

Julian had already disappeared inside. I took that as a good omen, because then I might have been lucky enough not to see him for the rest of the evening. We sat down at a circular bar and within minutes were surrounded by several attractive people. Both men and women. They smelled very eroticizing and intoxicating. I downed drink after drink, trying to build up my courage. So I loosened up and I let my eyes wander through the crowd.

My gaze lingered on a person who attracted me like magic. He was tall. Very tall. Almost two metres. His hair was white blond and his eyes were ice blue. He wore black tight pants and a white shirt. His pecs were clearly visible underneath. I felt him eyeing me as well. Interested. Scrutinising. Through a sea of people, his tall attractive figure pushed his way toward me. Everyone seemed to make room for him. Seconds later, he was standing in front of me and I had to crane my neck to look into his eyes. If I didn't know better, I'd say he looked like a Viking.

"You're the birthday girl?", I heard his sonorous voice and swallowed hard.

"Yeah. How did you know?", I said, stammering slightly. This guy was already making me nervous as hell.

"I'm the owner of this club and I know everything. Call me Erik. I hope you know what to do in a swingers club..." he smiled at me through his gleaming white teeth and held out his hand. I grasped his long slender pale fingers and it shot through me like lightning. It tingled throughout my body.

"Yeah, sure. Sex with other people's partners. Partner swapping," I stammered sheepishly, looking down at the floor.

"So, is your friend here in the room?"

"No, he isn't. I'm here with friends," I said sheepishly and let out a deep sigh.

"Do you want to take your friends with you, or do you want to make do with me and my people?" he asked me in a commanding voice.

"I like meeting new people. " I looked up at Erik and his eyes looked at me promptly.

"Perfect. I'll have Sookie and Demi come. You'll love them," he said and we walked together, under the curious gaze of the others, to the back of the club and up a curved spiral staircase.

Once upstairs, many doors opened and we went through a wide double door. This room was large and not at all as gloomy as I had imagined. A wide double bed with white sheets stood in the middle of the room and from there another door led off into a spacious bathroom with marble tiles.

"Do you like it? This is my private space," he grabbed my body and hugged me to him.

He smelled sensual and erotic. There was suddenly an incredible erotic tension in the room and he leaned down to me. His lips were only a few inches away from mine. Then he took my hand and slid it down his pants. I wrenched my eyes open and gasped heavily as I felt his erect penis in my hand. I reached for it, clutching it tightly, and he closed his eyes in pleasure. I opened his pants and freed his best piece. It stretched out towards me and I knelt on the floor. I ran my tongue once to the left and once to the right of his penis and touched his glans with the tip of my finger. Then I put my lips over his glans and pressed them together.

"Mia, I get a blowjob from you that fast?" he moaned, pressing my head against his cock.

I, completely inspired by what I was doing, sucked and sucked as best I could. I licked the tip, pressed with the other hand firmly around his penis and let this slide again and again all the way back into my throat. Faster and deeper until I was gagging slightly. My Viking's thighs tightened and he moaned louder. Then I bit down carefully with my teeth and with a yelp he squirted into my mouth and the warm salty liquid ran down my throat. It tasted very salty and I frowned for a moment. Then I stood up and looked Erik in the eyes and licked my lips with pleasure.

"I love it when you give me a blowjob so readily," he murmured to me, then pushed me against the edge of the bed.

"You're so fucking divine...", I sighed as his fingers slid inside my pants and played around with my clit.

"So wet, so tender, so ready," he moaned into my mouth as he kissed me passionately.

I felt another stirring in him as well. *Wow! The man was just bursting with testosterone!*

Then he pulled a condom out of his pocket, put it over himself and tore off my dress and panties. This I kicked on the floor and he lifted me with ease on his arms and I wrapped my legs around his hips. Then he pushed me against the wall and rammed his penis into my vulva. I gasped briefly as this was so big it filled me completely and moaned loudly. His eyes were dark with lust and desire and then he pushed my hips against him again and again with fast hard movements and fucked me harder and faster.

"Oh please, take me! ", I moaned and pressed my lips to his mouth.

Then I heard a knock on the door and jerked my head around. My heartbeat pounded all the way to my throat and I quivered with desire. I saw two beautiful women walk in. It had to be Sookie and Demi. Both were stark naked. One had angelic long blonde hair down to her hips, the other jet black shoulder length wavy hair. Both were incredibly beautiful.

"I'm Sookie," the blonde introduced herself.

"I'm Demi," the black-haired girl purred, then started stroking my belly with her fingers.

I sucked in a sharp breath and felt a thousand butterflies flutter in my stomach as Sookie then pressed her lips to mine and slid her other hand down to my pubic. She played with my clit, pulling on it and pushing me down onto the bed. Erik stood by, looking greedily like a hungry wolf at the game we three women were offering him. I closed my eyes with pleasure and gasped when she slid a finger inside me.

"You are so sensual and so receptive to any kind of touch. We like to have customers like that in our club Mia," Sookie moaned, lowered herself to her knees in front of me, spread my legs wide apart and already her tongue had disappeared in my vulva.

Relentlessly and demanding she licked my labia, pushed her tongue tip deep inside me and firmly embraced my ass. I did not know what happened to me and just wanted to savour this new form of love and passion to the fullest. I pushed my hips towards her and moaned once more as Sookie slid two more fingers inside me and fingered me so hard I could hardly hear or see. Faster and faster and more and more intensely her tongue sped out of me and back in. I kneaded my own breasts harder and harder and played with my own nipples with pleasure. Then Sookie slid even further under me, pushing my legs even further apart, and I felt a finger inside my anus. This slid in and out again, over and over. She fingered my ass from underneath so relentlessly that I groaned loudly, pushing my vulva deep into her face as she did so.

"Fuck me faster Sookie, please...", I murmured to her.

"Come for me Mia, let it all out," Sookie gasped, looking up at me with her innocent eyes and that's when I couldn't hold on any longer and exploded over her, moaning her name loudly into the room.

I felt completely exhausted, but then Erik came again and gave me no time to catch my breath. He pushed my back forward from behind so that my ass stretched out towards him. He clasped it, stroked my anus with one finger, and slid a finger inside me. I gasped and when he stuck a second finger in my ass I was overcome by a wave of pleasure.

"Fuck me in the ass, come on! ", I pressed out.

"Your ass does invite it, my dear Mia," he moaned, positioning himself in front of it and then sliding his penis into my anus. It squeezed for a brief moment, I pressed my lips tightly together. Then it was just horny. He moved faster and harder, thrusting his penis into my anus all the way to the shaft, and I satisfied myself with my other hand on my wet pussy. I wanted to feel it properly on both holes and fingered myself until I was completely filled with lust.

"Let me pleasure your pussy, you don't have to do everything yourself on your birthday Mia," Demi said, tossing her long black hair back, sitting down next to me and sliding her fingers against my vulva. She spread my lips and rubbed three of her fingers firmly against my pubic area.

"Oh my god, don't torture me like this...", I gasped, more than aroused, and pressed my lips together.

Demi's fingers sought their way into my hole and sank in. I was so wet and moist that she kept sliding out of me and entering me harder. Erik continued to thrust into my anus hard from behind and I held on convulsively in the sheets. He moaned loudly and his thrusts became faster and faster. Harder and harder until we both could no longer hold back and he squirted his juice into me. I also came with a loud cry and then sank trembling to my knees. I felt his still erect penis trembling inside me. His cum made its way up my ass and began to leak out. Down his penis. I let his cock slide out of my anus, turned around and sucked on it with relish. Licked his cum off his penis and took his thing in my mouth once more before slowly sliding it out and laying down for a moment. Erik lay down with the two of them with me.

"You are a remarkable woman. How old did you get?" Erik asked me, propping himself up next to me.

"Thirty. A horrible number." I let out a sigh, still needing to collect myself.

"Thirty is the new twenty. Remember that. Your golden years are yet to come. Trust me, I know what I'm talking about," Erik winked at me and then joined Sookie and Demi in the shower. I, on the other hand, quickly got dressed and disappeared back into the club. There I partied with my friends until the wee hours of the morning and caught a deep, erotic look from Erik and the two girls every now and then.

Best birthday ever...

Group Sex with my jock Friends

I closed my eyes for a moment. I enjoyed her touch. It was so gentle and yet intense.

"Your skin is flawless. You look like you've been kissed by the sun. Not pale like all of us here. You're like the sun that came here to our training centre," she breathed into my ear and ran her index finger over my lips.

Then she grabbed my hand and pulled me with her under the shower. The water jet pelted down on us and Lena pressed me against the wall. She pressed her lips to mine, pressed her tongue between my lips and sought mine. Her hands clasped my ass and I wrapped my arms around her neck. It felt so good to have her with me.

"I saw you dancing and I knew right away I wanted you," she gasped between our kisses.

"I felt the same way. I saw you and I was enchanted. You are so beautiful, like a little elf from an enchanted forest," I said, holding her heart-shaped face in my hands.

"I want you. Now! ", Lena said and ran her hand down to my pubic area.

There she pressed my thighs apart and stroked my labia with her index finger. I closed my eyes again with pleasure and then inhaled audibly when she pushed her finger inside me. But I wanted to pleasure her too, so my kisses moved down her neck and down to her breasts. I sucked tenderly on her nipples, licking and pulling on them. Her mouth was slightly open, she was breathing heavily. It pleased Lena, how beautiful. She slid a second and third finger inside me, working my pussy hard and relentlessly. Her movements became faster and faster. I pressed my lower body against her hand and went rhythmically along.

"Oh yes, please, faster...", I moaned, begging for more.

Lena lowered herself to her knees and began circling my clit with her tongue.

"You're so wet, after me," Lena breathed, letting her tongue keep circling clockwise.

She stretched my vulva further and further, her tongue drove in and out again. My pussy quivered with desire and I threw my head back. She pushed my legs further apart until she was directly under me and then rubbed her mouth against my anus. Faster and harder. Back and forth between vulva and anus. I almost lost my breath and gave one short cry of desire. My legs became stiff and began to tremble.

"I'm about to cum... In a minute...", I gasped out, and then a wave of pleasure rolled over me.

I literally soared into the sky and landed on a wave of bliss. Then I sank to the ground and breathed deeply in and out to calm myself down again. Then I stood up again and looked mischievously at Lena.

"What's wrong Toni?" she asked me and then took a long shower.

"There's a gentleman from the dance academy coming to see us today. He decides who gets to come to the States and get the scholarship...", I started to talk.

"Toni, why are you worrying right now... You're going to be his first choice anyway. So keep your cool. You're the best dancer I know and everyone knows it," Lena reassured me, giving me a final wink as she left me alone.

All of us girls lived in a large dormitory near the dance studio where we had our performances. Today was a very special day for all of us. For me, too, of course. Because today it was decided who would get the big scholarship to the American Dance Academy. This was a milestone in every dancer's career. I shared a small room with wooden bunk beds with three other girls. Two were sixteen years old, my good friend Lena and I were eighteen. We put on our tracksuits and patted our feet. Because by now my feet were plagued with constant pain. Like I said, success comes at a price and you had to sacrifice everything. Even your health. Was that normal or right? I don't know. In competitive sports, there is no normal or abnormal. There's no right or wrong. You live a different life and you live your dream.

Once we were dressed and had our long hair pulled back into a tight bun, we walked down to the breakfast room dressed in our tracksuits. It was a sparse room with white plastic tables and bright neon lights. Don't expect a big buffet or anything like that now. As I said before, we had to watch our figure. On our table was a big glass carafe with lemon water. Along with that, there was a low-fat cereal for each of us and low-fat protein bars for the road in case we got too hungry. It wasn't until the evening that we got to look forward to another meal. Low calorie of course. That's just the way it was. I poked around listlessly in my cereal again and tried to concentrate on today.

"Calm down Toni. Stay cool as always and convince the headhunter about you." Whispered Lena and stroked tenderly over my thigh.

"You know very well Toni that you are one of the best dancers of us. Only Svetlana could still get in the way of your dream. Otherwise, I can't think of many others who dance as perfectly as you do," Lena replied and poked me in the side.

"I'll try my best. I won't let anyone take this great opportunity away from me, no matter the cost," I pressed out between clenched teeth, clenching my hands into fists so that it hurt. But I was used to pain.

When we arrived at our dressing room, there was already a huge bustle. I quickly put on my short tight shorts and a belly top. I hurriedly ran with the other girls through the halls and to the back of the rehearsal room and did my warm-ups along with them.. I just needed to focus on me today. As I was lost in thought doing my exercises a little further off to the side, I didn't even notice someone watching me. The person was standing next to the big dance mirror and leaning against a wall. He had a small notepad in his hand and was writing some things down. His eyes wandered from one girl to the next and kept lingering on me. As I practiced a pirouette, spinning around several times, I caught out of the corner of my eye our dance instructor Elijah talking to the person and they pointed at me. I had had my eye on my instructor for a long time. He was so damn hot, but I had always been too shy to approach him because he was definitely ten years older than me. Plus, he was kind of my boss and I didn't want to mess with Elijah under any circumstances.

"Toni, why don't you come over here and join us," Elijah called out, waving at me.

I hurriedly walked over to the two and was now able to properly examine the person standing next to him for the first time. It was a tall man, had a slim figure, jet black hair and striking facial features. His grass-green eyes examined me from top to bottom and without thinking anything of it, he even walked around me twice. Like a lion surveying its prey. It felt a bit like being in a bazaar. As if one were a commodity. Then he stood directly in front of me and held out his hand.

"Toni, this is Christian. He's the head of the Dance Academy of Los Angeles and I told him that you and Svetlana are our two best dancers," Elijah introduced me to him and I gave him my hand. When our hands touched I suddenly felt cold and hot at the same time. His hand was cool, yet soft and smooth. He squinted his eyes a little and took a deep breath.

"Toni Scott... A promising name and apparently a promising talent as well. I will be present at the rehearsals from now on and whichever of them is the better dancer tonight, I'll take her with me to Los Angeles tomorrow," he spoke in a velvety soft voice and my mood lifted to unimagined heights.

"Really? If I make it tonight then... Then you'll take me to America with you?" I asked, my mouth dry as dust.

"Yes. And not only that. Whoever wins here is going to be at the front of the pack for next year. It's going to be tough, very tough. But the one who makes it then is at the goal of their dreams. So give it your all, Toni. Be ready to make sacrifices, no matter what," he breathed to me and stroked my knuckles with his index finger. Again a pleasant shiver ran down my spine.

"Yes. I'll give it my all. Thank you, Christian. I won't let her down," I pressed out, looking into those beautiful eyes once more. His jaw muscles tightened and only reluctantly did he let go of my hand.

"I didn't expect anything else from them either," Christian whispered as he walked past me, Elijah following him as they were now heading straight for Svetlana and performing the same circus on her.

I looked jealously in her direction, as Svetlana was of course going all out, laughing bright as a bell and looking like she was about to do a lap dance number on Christian. I rolled my eyes in annoyance and then ran up to the stage... I danced. I danced for my life. I was focused on only one goal and that was America. I tensed my body, twisted in all directions and more and more of my fellow dancers came on stage and took their positions as well. Sweat was pouring off my forehead. My feet ached. My spine felt like it was about to snap and my arms were getting heavier and heavier. But I did not give up. I wanted to finish the number, because again I noticed that from the beginning Christian had sat down in the back of the hall and didn't let me out of his sight. He followed my every move. Nothing escaped him. Every now and then he pulled out his notepad or talked on his mobile phone. But his incredibly green eyes were still fixed on me. I also kept glancing in his direction. I wanted him to look at me. Wanted our eyes to meet. I wanted him to see that I was only dancing for him now.

Late in the afternoon I sat in the communal dressing room massaging my blue sore and slightly bleeding feet. I dipped them into a foot bath and winced as it burned and hurt so much. Lena came to me and put her arm around my shoulder.

"Tell me, what have you been up to today? You're dancing like your life depends on it. “

"It's my life Lena. I have to make it today. And I don't care what happens to me," I pressed out and squeezed my eyes shut in pain.

"Who was that handsome man who's been lurking around here since this morning? He was with us backup dancers, too, watching us," Lena asked, handing me a bottle of lemon water.

"Thanks," I sighed and took a big gulp. "This is Christian. He belongs to the Dance Academy of Los Angeles and either Svetlana or I get to go with him tomorrow," I told her and again I bit my lower lip because my feet hurt so much.

"What? Madness. Do you know what that means? You'd be at the destination of your dreams. Give it your all," Lena slapped her hands over her mouth and widened her eyes.

"That's just it. I've got to make it. Only my feet are going to kill me soon," I whined softly, choking back a tear. No, I couldn't cry now. There was no room for that.

"You can do this. You just have to try to believe in yourself and... Hey, this guy's hot. You have everything a man could ever want. So show him," Lena said, laughing out loud.

"Please? Just look at me. Pale, emaciated, far from big breasted and you can count the ribs on all of us. A top model has more fat on her ribs than we do," I sighed, looking down at my emaciated body.

"He knows that, though. I don't think girls look any different in America. Possibly even worse than us. Come on, grit your teeth and keep going," Lena cheered me on and I just nodded.

"You go ahead, I'll join you in a minute. I still have to bandage my feet," I said and seconds later I was alone.

I enjoyed the peace and quiet the dressing room gave me and then needily bandaged my feet. I looked at myself in the mirror for a moment and sighed. As I looked down at myself I heard the door click. Then I heard footsteps and recognized a man's stature in the reflection. It was Christian's. He stood only a few feet behind me and looked at me. His eyes were dark and there was a desire in them. Then I heard another click and my coach Elijah came into the dressing room as well.

"Christian? Elijah? Were they looking for me, am I late?", I asked, swallowing hard.

"We were looking for you Toni," Christian whispered softly and came very close to me. My heart was pounding in my throat and I could smell his scent. This one smelled tart and spicy. Absolutely arousing.

"I'll be right there. I know the audition is about to go on," I stammered and was about to turn around when his hand grabbed hold of my arm and with his other hand he gently stroked my arm. I shivered slightly and closed my eyes as he did so.

"We still have a moment. Toni, you're incredible. The best of them all. I've seen that from the beginning. There's just one more certain thing between you and getting into the really big business," Christian murmured in my ear and then kissed me gently along my neck. He brushed his hand along my stomach as he did so and then continued upwards to my breasts. I gasped when he ran his hand under my top and played with my nipples.

"Christian, I can't do this. I can't, not...", I whispered, fighting the urge inside.

"What can't you do? Cross a line for success? Don't think you're the first one willing to do that?" whispered Elijah suddenly, standing to my left.

He turned me around and looked me firmly in the face. There was hunger in his expression. Hunger for me. Hunger for my body. I took my face in his hands and then gently placed his lips on mine. He kissed me in no stormy way, but passionately and gently. Like I was fragile. Like a doll made of glass. I struggled, but I realised I was losing this battle. I lost myself in him. His smell, his look, his voice. Everything about Elijah was so inviting. Like a feast I hadn't had in a long time. I wanted it. I wanted it so badly. Then I buried my hands in his hair, tugging gently and playing with his tongue. He stripped off my clothes, loosening my hair, which fell down my back in jet black waves. I just stood there in front of them in my dancing shoes, breathing short and heavy.

"You look enchanting. Beautiful. Like a delicate little doll, but with tremendous strength and stamina. There is so much in you that I would still like to discover," Christian now said coming up to me and then grabbing my calf. Then he started to stretch my leg slowly upwards. Further and further until my foot came to a stop right next to my face. He walked a foot away from me and looked at me. Lustfully. Sensually. Impressed by what he was seeing.

"I want you now. Stay like that," he sucked in a sharp breath and pulled off his pants.

His gaze was fixed on me. As Christian stripped off his boxers, I could examine his penis in its full glory and I noticed how the sight of me excited him. I felt - powerful. Triumphant. Victorious. Then he knelt in front of me, my right leg still extended in the air, and he ran his fingers over my vulva, which stretched out to meet him. I shuddered as he slid a finger inside me and then slid his tongue over my aroused labia.

"God in heaven, you are so beautiful and so unspent Toni," he moaned out between his tongue play and I slowly tensed up as I felt a lust inside me and had to concentrate at the same time not to fall over.

Again and again first one finger and then a second slid into me and his tongue slid over my clit and stimulated me to the extreme. Then he reached around my hips and pressed his whole tongue deep into my vulva and sucked, licked and kissed me until my lower abdomen tightened and I came loudly with a sigh, pressing his head even harder against my pubic.

I gasped and shivered as I put my leg back down on the floor beside me, and Christian's face was heated and full of passion for me.

"Now it's my turn. I want you! Now! I've wanted this for a long time," moaned Elijah, who had closed his hand around his penis and was pleasuring himself.

"Where?", I gave a short breath, still enjoying the aftershock of my orgasm.

"Here, stand against the wall. Bend over as far as you can, and I know you can do it far and deep..." there was a commanding tone in Elijah's voice.

I obeyed. I turned my back on him, spread my legs and bent forward down until my palms were on the cold hard stone floor of the locker room. I heard Elijah draw in air behind me and he groaned as he positioned himself behind me and then thrust firmly into me.

"Ah!" I exclaimed loudly, feeling his penis fill me completely.

Elijah started fucking me relentlessly from behind with hard firm thrusts faster and harder. He held my shoulder and with the other hand clutched my hips and pushed hard.

"Fuck Toni, you're tight," he gasped under each thrust and I felt my legs tighten again.

Then Christian stood directly in front of me, lifted my chin up with his hand and I looked at his erect penis, which almost moved in my face. I licked my lips provocatively, opened my mouth and Christian pushed his member into my mouth. I sucked and sucked, gripping his shaft tightly with one hand and tonguing his glans over and over. Christian moved his hips in my direction and literally fucked my mouth. From behind, I additionally felt Elijah slide a wet finger into my tight ass. In, out and in again and out again. He was getting faster and faster and I was getting hornier and hornier.

"Oh, what's happening? Can I join in too?" we suddenly heard a voice and paused in our position.

It was Lena. She slid out from behind the locker in the changing room and was flaming red in the face. Heated from what we were doing. Ignoring Elijah and Christian, she slid under me, took Christian's cock in her hand and pulled it out of my wet pussy with one tug.

"I want to lick that one. Put it in her ass. Toni is particularly into that," whispered Lena and I already felt her tongue in my vulva again.

I moaned loudly and continued to lick Elijah's penis.

"Such a hot ass he wants to be fucked from behind too," I heard Christian's rough voice and he positioned himself behind me and how my ass wanted it.

With a jolt, I was catapulted forward and clung to Elijah's thighs as Christian entered my anus from behind. It hurt briefly and I winced. But then he moved rhythmically inside me and I cried out loudly. Lena's tongue play kept sending little shivers through my body and I felt like I was going to explode. I rested my head on the back of my neck and moaned out as I tensed to the utmost. Elijah grabbed my head and pushed his penis into my mouth again. One last time, Christian thrust his cock deep inside me and poured into me with a yelp. His penis jerked wildly inside me and I moaned loudly again. Elijah also could not hold on any longer and then squirted his sperm deep into my throat. I felt his cock deep in my mouth and he fucked my mouth for a while longer before I slumped to the floor and stayed there for a few minutes. All strength had gone out of my body and I felt like I was in sex heaven.

"Toni, you're an absolute grenade. Please dance tonight just for us! Prove it to everyone that you are the best dancer and deserve to win," Christian spoke, then pulled me up and kissed me on the hands and then on the mouth.

Since then, not a day went by that I didn't miss dancing when I wasn't doing it. By now I was at home on the big stages of the world. Because every dancer in the world would agree with me: The love of dance eclipses any other form of love. And if you can't dance once, it's as if a part of your soul is missing.

A Gangbang with Beauties

Frustrated, I looked at my hair in the mirror. It just did not want to fall over my back today as I thought it would. Even blow-drying and perpetual straightening didn't help. Finally I let it down. I looked a bit like Snow White, as I was just missing the summer tan this year. I was back home in New York for a few days off. I was thirty-eight years old and worked for a software company in sales. My family and I lived in a small townhouse in Manhattan, a very well-to-do area of New York City.

In my job there were few days off and therefore I tried to enjoy them to the fullest. My husband Frederic was once again at a congress and our nanny Monica had gone shopping. My son Jackson was in school until the afternoon, so I had time to take care of myself again.

Lost in thought, I strolled to my wardrobe, which I had finally rearranged yesterday and picked out halfway decent clothes for today. I decided on a pair of tight jeans and a white blouse with lace holes. Then I shouldered my bag and walked out of my room down the hall and threw on my denim jacket. I looked at my iPhone again and sighed, as several emails were piling up in my inbox again. But I had sworn not to work on my days off. Otherwise I would get a burn-out.

I looked around and then walked down the long boulevard. Very close to our house was a Starbucks and this lifted my mood every day. Therefore, with my iPhone in hand, I strolled into the cosy coffee shop. There, I joined the queue and typed boredly on my phone. I was once again completely lost in thought that I didn't even notice how I was suddenly jostled from behind and almost tipped over to the front.

"Excuse me, watch it!", I turned around to the back and looked at a young man's chest.

This one was at least two heads taller than me and looked at me somewhat amused from above. He had crystal blue eyes like me, but jet black hair, which was cut accurately and a light three-day beard. He wore black pants, a white shirt, and a leather jacket over it. A tart sweet scent emanated from him. I sucked this in and it almost befuddled my senses. Erotic.

"Sorry kiddo, but I guess I missed you," he just shrugged in amusement, flashing me his toothpaste smile.

"Kiddo? Don't call me that, I'm probably a lot older than you. So watch your tongue," I returned bitingly, turning around and just looking annoyed at the coffee bar.

"Oh my god you're bitchy. You must be in desperate need of a guy again, huh?", I heard him say and I widened my eyes. Then I turned around again and glared at him.

"Look, bug someone else with your talk, but shut the fuck up already. I don't want to have anything to do with guys like you," I drove at him with a raised index finger, threw my long dark hair back into my neck and then simply stomped past the crowd and ordered my coffee.

I did get nasty looks from other customers, but I didn't care. I just wanted to get out. Seconds later, I was standing in the street with my heart pounding, looking up at the sky for a moment to regain my composure. What was that just now? The day was off to a good start. I took a big gulp of coffee and then headed downtown, shaking my head, to do a little shopping. I also ran into my best friend Leila. She also worked at the same software company, but in accounting. Leila also had a son, but he was already in college. She was divorced and also had on and off changing acquaintances. I couldn't blame her. Together we strolled through the mall and chatted about this and that.

"Are you hungry? I'm in the mood for a pizza or something right now," Leila said, looking at me with her loyal eyes. She was a little shorter than me, had red hair and a heart-shaped face. She seemed younger and more childlike than she actually was.

"Yeah, sure. I'm in on everything. I know a cute little pizza place, at least it tastes good there," I said and pointed in that direction.

We placed our order and sat down at a small table by the window front.

"Would you like to go out partying again this weekend? We haven't done that for ages and I think it's about time again," Leila asked me.

"All right, and where to? And who's all coming, or did you want to go in pairs?"

"I would take my friend Alex, she's always fun to hang out with and Taylor. Taylor is a mutual friend of ours. He takes a little getting used to sometimes, but otherwise he's nice. We'll pick you up. Is that okay?", Leila asked me as we walked to the exit after dinner.

"Yeah, whatever. Maybe I need a change of pace too. It certainly doesn't hurt," I sighed heavily and we said goodbye.

In the evening, I had made myself a little nervous. I hadn't been out for a long time, as I was usually so tied up with work that I just didn't have the time or energy. As I stepped out the front door in my knee length black dress, I saw my taxi. Loud techno came from the silver grey SUV with tinted windows and I immediately remembered my first party trips. However, I was seventeen at the time. I slid into the back seat with Leila. Up front at the wheel was this guy Alex and next to him was a hip young woman.

"Hi Carrie, Hi Leila. Carrie, I'm Taylor, a college friend of Alex's. Don't worry, I drive properly," he said, motioning his upper body forward.

"Hi Taylor, well then I'm reassured," I replied kindly, biting my lower lip.

"You can depend on Taylor's driving skills Carrie. After all, we are all over thirty and know how to behave while driving and at parties. But today we're really going for it again," Alex winked at me and my senses sparked.

We drove criss-cross through several streets and the loud music, which had changed from techno to hard rock, soon made my ears ring. We crossed the Harlem River and the streets here no longer looked quite as posh and distinguished as I was used to them. Then I saw lights of a big stadium. The stadium of the Yankees and I looked at Leila a bit horrified from the side.

"Leila? Don't tell me we're not in Manhattan anymore?"

"We're not in Manhattan anymore," she said with a shrug.

"Where are we going?", I asked her, already about to pull out my iPhone to call Stuart.

"Keep your iPhone in your pocket Carrie. We're in the Bronx going to the hip Hard Rock Cafe." I heard Alex's voice and she turned around beaming.

"Bronx? Now that's not my favourite part of town," I pressed out and slid deeper into my seat.

"The Bronx doesn't equal the Bronx where violence, drugs, and alcohol rule. Jump over your shadow Upper East Side girl," Taylor said and I looked into his dark eyes in the rearview mirror. "I already know why I can't relate to you rich people. You guys have lost all sense of reality and only know the words Prada, Gucci and the like. I think that's very sad," Taylor said, turning into the street where Yankee Stadium and our destination was.

Countless crowds of people bustled on the sidewalks. It was loud, it was shrill, and people kept bumping into you. I kept close to Leila and we walked behind Taylor and Alex.

"Did we order a lounge?", I asked Leila and once again Taylor turned to look at me.

"A lounge? Oh, sorry princess. I only made a reservation for one table, which wasn't easy on a Friday night anyway. However, I figured that probably wouldn't be enough for a woman of your standing," he said, annoyed.

"Tell me, do you have something against me?", I asked him straightforwardly, stepping up beside him as we pulled up in front of the entrance to the Hard Rock Cafe. A line of people stood there waiting. Lots of young people in strange clothes. Some looked like punks, some looked like rockers, and some looked like hippies. I really felt completely out of place.

"I explained to you before in the car that I actually can't stand people like you who always think they're better just because of their money." His dark eyes fixed on me and his almost black hair stood out a bit.

"I don't feel like I'm any better. I'm just used to a different standard in my life. And you should know that I grew up in a normal neighbourhood in Brooklyn and my parents are middle class. I worked hard to earn my current standard of living." I snarled at him by now, my eyes flashing. My long black hair blew in the breeze of the evening air and my heartbeat sped up.

"Whatever. We can go in. If you have a reservation you don't have to wait in line," Taylor sighed, pushing me in front of her like a little girl.

Inside it was packed and we pushed our way through a mass of people. Immediately the smell of cheap shower gel and perfume hit my nose and the smell of sweat. On the walls were many pictures of rock stars and countless guitars. Our table was near the bar and I settled down on the cream-colored couch, which I quickly eyed in return. Was that really why I was a bad aloof person?

"What do you want to drink?" asked Alex quickly to the group, sensing that the air was a little tense between me and Taylor.

"Cosmopolitan," I said without looking at the menu.

"I'll have a Cosmo too," Leila said quickly in my defense.

"Figures," Taylor grumbled, ordering a beer for himself and Alex. "You guys want something to eat too?"

"A burger and fries please..." I said, nodding to the waitress who quickly scribbled this on her pad.

"Burgers and fries? Seriously?" Taylor asked me, looking taken aback.

"Guess what, I went to high school and college once too and I know what they eat. I didn't just grow up on shrimp and champagne," I sighed, stroking my hair and then letting my eyes wander around the diner so I wouldn't have to talk to Taylor about me and my lifestyle.

At first I didn't notice them at all, but then their appearances like red dots just stood out from the crowd. My gaze lingered on a small group of people who were on the other side of the pub. They were sitting at a round table, but they didn't seem to be talking much. Sometimes they would exchange a few words and then they would all stare off into space again. I felt as if everyone else standing around them was vying for their favour.

There were two boys and a girl. The girl looked like a classic beauty. Her hair was fawn and fell in long waves down to her hips. She wore washed out jeans and a snow white sweater. Her face was elf-like. The boy next to her was a little stockier, broad-shouldered, and had muscles like an active weightlifter. He wore black jeans, also ragged, and a red t-shirt with a skull print. He also had tattoos on his arms. His hair was short and blond. Then my eyes wandered to the third person at the table and it almost hit me like a bolt of lightning. I stared at him as if spellbound. He was tall in stature, slightly muscular but not as extreme as his table mate. His skin was lightly tanned, like a golden glow. His hair had a mixture of blonde and brown, like the colour from a star hairdresser. However, I was sure he had never visited a star hairdresser. He was wearing washed out dark blue jeans, a black shirt, and a leather jacket over it. He kept sipping a beer bottle and looked a little grumpy. Leila noticed how my gaze had been glued to these three people for a few minutes and nudged me from the side.

"Hey Carrie, you okay?"

"Yeah, sure. I was just thinking," I said and quickly turned back to my Cosmo.

"See anything you like?" laughed Alex, joining us on the bench as Taylor was engrossed in conversation with a friend he probably knew.

"Not really. I just noticed a few people, that's all," I shrugged and lowered my head.

"Come on tell me, who caught your eye? ", Leila asked theatrically and clapped her hands.

"Not so loud. Everyone doesn't have to know I'm here," I whispered, making myself even smaller than I already was.

"I can't imagine that anyone would expect to see you here. So, come on...", Alex urged and looked around with interest.

"Who are they back there?", I asked, nodding back over to the small group who had just ordered a portion of fries.

"Who?" asked Alex, cocking his head.

"The ones back there by the window, at the round table. The ones eating fries right now. The two guys and the girl," I said, looking over at them again.

"Oh, them. It's the Gents. You stay away from them. They're not good company for you. Don't come from a good household," Alex whispered, shaking her head and her red hair a mess.

"Aha, who are they? Crack dealers and pimps?", I asked amused and drank my Cosmo empty.

"Something like that. They belong to a gang that's been running wild in this area. They've been involved in some criminal activity. The police are always dealing with them. All three of them go to college nearby. They're bright kids, but they seem to run afoul of the law. My son has a lot of run-ins with them. Besides, they're way too young for us, and you're married. So, stay away from them," Alex told her and Leila nodded in agreement.

"I wasn't planning on talking to them or anything like that either. I just noticed them because they were just..."

"Damn good looking? Yeah, you're not the only one who thinks so. The girl's name is Mary-Jane, but everyone just calls her M.J. The boy who looks like a bodybuilder, that's Jack. The one next to him is his younger brother Aaron. Anything else you wanna know about them? If there is, I'll ask my son. He goes to college with them and I think he's taking some classes with Aaron," Leila told me and then sat back and relaxed.

"How old are they?", I asked curiously, my gaze still fixed on Aaron Gent. I found him handsome. Incredibly attractive.

"Early twenties, like most people who go to college. I think the Gents have repeated a year before, too. I don't know. Like I said, if you want to know more, I'll ask my son," Leila stood up and then walked over to the bar without another word.

"I need to go to the bathroom. Keep my seat warm Alex," I called into her ear as the music had gotten a little louder and then weaved my way through the crowds towards the restrooms.

My path inevitably led me past the Gents' table and just as I spotted the restroom sign, a big guy bumped into me from the side and I almost fell into their table. Just then a pair of strong arms caught me and immediately I sucked in a beguiling smell. Masculine. Tart. Erotic. Alluring. Those words inevitably popped into my head and I looked into a pair of amber eyes. It went through me anew like a lightning bolt and I got goosebumps. I lifted my head and was set back on both feet.

"I didn't realise the older and damn attractive women were already falling for me. Did you Jack?", I heard a voice firm yet smooth.

"Must have slipped my mind Aaron," the boy named Jack said, eyeing me.

My "saviour" Aaron also scanned me from top to bottom and I suddenly felt so... Naked. I tugged restlessly at my black dress and tossed my long black hair back on my neck. My teeth chewed on my bottom lip and my mouth went dry as dust as well. Seconds passed. Endless seconds and I lost myself in those stunning caramel colored eyes of Aaron. He too looked at me for quite a while until he sat back down and took a sip of his beer. I wanted to keep walking, but my legs just weren't doing what I was asking them to do. Then suddenly the model-like Mary-Kate turned to me and eyed me as well.

"She's really damn good looking. It's rare to see someone like you around here, and we're around a lot. You must be from the Upper East Side, right?" the young woman across from me asked.

“Yes, something like that. Sorry, I didn't mean to disturb you," I stammered, slightly embarrassed. My self-confidence was completely in the basement.

"Cool. I like you. Don't you want to be with us for a little bit?", Aaron asked me again and pulled me towards him once more.

"I don't know if that's such a good idea. I'm way too old for you guys, too."

"Old? What is it with you all and age? You're hotter than some of the twenty year old women in this pub," Jack said and sat down close to us.

"I think you're totally hot too. Do you want to play a game with us? We don't bite either. What's your name?" Mary-Jane breathed in my ear. I hadn't even noticed that all three of them had moved in close to me. Their manner, their scents...everything about them drew me in like magic. I felt trapped. Like I was completely drugged. It was intoxicating.

"My name is Carrie...", I stammered, my pulse accelerating more and more.

Then I stood up as if in a trance and just let these three complete strangers accompany me towards the toilets. The toilets were spacious and even as I stood in front of one of the sinks, the handsome young guy named Aaron pressed up against me. I let out a sigh as his hand moved to my panties and disappeared into them. Before I knew it I felt his fingers on my vagina, gently caressing it and with his other hand he gently kneaded my breasts. Seconds later he slid three fingers inside me and I gasped.

"Oh, please, don't torture me like this," I groaned between my teeth and put my head back.

"I love hearing women like you moan. You're so hot," he said, then jerked me around to face him. His breath had quickened. He slid his fingers into my mouth and I sucked on them lustfully.

"I want you to undress me now," he ordered me quietly, looking at me with a commanding expression. "That's the effect you have on me," Aaron said, taking my hand and placing it on his erection.

I swallowed hard and tightened my grip around his member. He closed his eyes. I took off Aaron's pants and also his boxers. His penis was very large, had a beautiful pink colour and stood like a one.

"Aaron, let us have a go too. Here beautiful, how do you like my cock?" the bigger of the two, Jack, whispered in my ear and I looked down at his big pale pink penis. I was numb and not aware of anything around me. I just sucked in the erotic scents emanating from the three of them.

Jack leaned against the sink with pleasure, pushed his pelvis far forward and I knelt down. I then took his penis in my mouth, close my lips tightly around it and start sucking hard and licking up and down his glans with my tongue. Under me his hips begin to twitch.

"You women and your divine mouth work. There's nothing better," Jack moaned and gasped.

I felt so powerful. It was an amazing feeling. Blowjobs gave a woman the feeling to have everything in hand. His body became stiff as a rock and I let my mouth slide up and down again and again, my lips pressed together very tightly, over and over again.

Then I felt a hand on my ass and drove around briefly. Behind me squatted the beautiful M. J. and stroked my ass, then licked with pleasure over the index finger and inserted it into my anus. I gasped out loud, then Jack gently but firmly pushed my head in the direction of his penis and fucked my mouth. I closed my lips tighter around his member, trying to push my hips towards Mary-Jane's fingers at the same time, and felt a rising lust and passion deep inside me.

"Stop it Carrie! I want to fuck you before I cum," I sat up breathlessly and he looked at me with wide eyes. "Your enthusiasm completely disarms me and I almost came in your wonderful mouth," he gasped and then kissed me deeply.

"Now sit on top of me. I want to be deep inside you and feel every inch of your stunning body," he said with a smile, lifting me up with his arms and sliding right under me onto the cool floor tiles.

Slowly he penetrated me and I was almost breathless. His penis filled me completely and I moaned loudly. Seconds later he was completely inside me. Then he started to move inside me, holding my hips tightly and pushing me up and down again and again. Groaning, I put my head back on my neck and start to move as well. Both of our breaths come in bursts. Faster and faster. He lifted his pelvis and lowered it again. I was so wet and damp after him that everything inside me melted away.

But then I felt two more hands around my hips and I sucked in Aaron's scent. I couldn't see him, but I could smell him. He smelled so intoxicating, so alluring. It was like a drug. My own personal drug. All three of them.

"What a hot ass, Christmas came early," Aaron said, running his fingers over my ass the next moment he had me by the hair gently but firmly grabbed, pulled me back and then thrust hard. Anal, of course. It tightened briefly, but then I felt only horny. I had sex with two of the most beautiful men I had ever seen. And both were actually much too young for me.

"Yes, fuck me hard please Aaron," I cried out and was literally thrust forward. Then his thrusts started getting harder and harder. Faster and faster.

Then I looked down at M. J.'s long slender legs and glanced at her shaved pussy, which was right in front of my mouth.

"Carrie, if my brothers are going to fuck you, I want to be licked by you. Here..." she gasped, pressing her vagina to my lips. She was so soft, so wet, and so beautiful. I slid my tongue past her labia and pressed it against her clit and then into her vulva.

"So tight, so wet, so willing," Aaron gasped, fucking me relentlessly from behind. I came, screaming words without rhyme or reason. Jack also grasped my hips again, thrust into me hard a few more times, I put my head back in my neck and he too climaxed, but silently, and poured himself completely inside me.

Breathing heavily and with my heart pounding in my chest, I sank down on top of Jack and felt the warmth of Aaron against my back. I looked down at Mary-Jane's endless legs and reviewed everything.

"We don't usually get involved with anyone so quickly, but you... you're very special. What, we'll find out. Hope to see you again soon Carrie," Aaron said, getting dressed and kissing my forehead again. Jack and M.J. looked at me again for a moment and then walked out without another word.

That was the last time I saw these three beauties. I had been in the pub a few more times with my girlfriend, but they never showed up again.

A sinful Interview among Women

Stell had been in the fashion industry for a long time, in her early thirties and an editor of a small fashion magazine. But by now she wanted more and had applied for a job that was to be the triumph of her career. The famous underwear label *Agent Provocateur* was looking for a new editor for their magazine. Stell felt called to it and had immediately called there and submitted her documents.

Stell came from the rural area of Wales, pretty much on the coast of England, but she was always drawn to the metropolis of London. There she wanted to make a career for herself. After graduating, she had done fashion marketing at college with a grade one. She then travelled to Paris to stay with relatives and did a year-long internship at a fashion magazine. Here she got deep insights and was allowed to accompany the editor-in-chief several times to different fashion shows, met editors, models, designers... It was a dream.

It was her dream. Stell wanted to dive into this world, at any price. The highlight for Stell were the shows of the underwear models. When Stell sat in the front row of the fashion show in Paris with her editor and saw these beautiful, just-perfect leggy women float down the runway, she was smitten. These women had no flaws. Their long manes shone like gold in the sun. These hairstyles must have cost over six thousand dollars from the star hairdresser. Their skin was clear and lightly tanned from self-tanner. They wore a hint of nothing and floated down the catwalk to the music of a pop star. Their breasts were plump, round and their bottoms so toned and tight that Stell had to swallow harder every time she looked at them. But it was not only her. Numerous women and men were transfixed, staring at these young women as they floated past them. From that moment on, Stell had set her mind on wanting to work for this company so that she could be as close to these women as possible. After a few years and constantly fighting for different jobs at different fashion magazines and fashion labels, Stell had finally found her chance at an advertisement.

On the morning in question, she nervously rummaged around in her wardrobe and picked out a cream-colored pantsuit, black pumps and she curled her long jet-black hair with a curling iron. Add to that mascara and it was perfect. A quick glance in the mirror told her that it would have to fit like that and hopefully the people in HR wouldn't judge her hiring just on her appearance. After all, she had insanely good credentials and references to show for it. She grabbed her apartment key, purse, iPhone and quickly walked out of the apartment.

When Stell awkwardly entered the entrance hall, she was almost blinded by the slender, tall women and men who were running around a bit hectically, talking strained, talking on the phone or carrying clothes from A to B. She also didn't know that everyone here only answered to the name Prada! Nor did she know that everyone here only went by the names Prada! Versace! Armani! or Lagerfeld! It was a world of its own. A world in which she desperately wanted to arrive.

A group of leggy, spindly young women streamed to the elevators, chatting animatedly. Their feet were in shingled pumps and their spiked heels clacked on the marble floor. These women just looked forbiddingly good. Their plump round butts filled out the extremely tight pants perfectly. Their round breasts were literally popping out of the tops and through some you could see the pale pink nipples shining through. How she would love to have some private time with one or the other. Touch them, caress them, lick those beautiful bodies like a popsicle... Then a shiver ran through her and her abdomen tightened. She loved women. Women were just more exciting, more enigmatic, and much more sensual than men. Usually more difficult, too, but she loved a challenge. Sex with a woman was more exhausting, because to properly satisfy a woman took a lot more than it did with a man. Men were just too easy going.

Stell walked behind a group of models and slipped into the arriving elevator behind them. As the door closed, she pressed herself against the wall and it went higher and higher - to the heights of Agent Provocateur's human resources department. As she rode, she relaxed a little and her eyes roamed over the figures of the young women. All of them looked like models. One more beautiful than the other. After what felt like an eternity, she arrived at the top floor of the HR department and headed for the waiting area. As she was about to sit down, she heard the clack of heels and looked up. A graceful willowy woman, who introduced herself as Luna, picked her up.

"So you'd like to start with us?" she asked as they walked past more elf-like creatures into a sparsely furnished office down the hall.

"Absolutely. It would be a great honour to work for this company," she said nervously.

"You are very qualified and I see you have fashion sense. That's promising, for a start. But whether you are really suited for the position of editor, I don't really know," Luna said and sat down at a desk with a white laptop in front of it.

She rested her head on her hands and looked at her penetratingly. Stell looked at Luna's full lips and noticed how she chewed on them slightly. Her breasts were extremely large and stretched her blouse. How she would love to take them in her hand and nibble on the nipples. Her pulse quickened slightly and she was completely lost in thought when Luna's voice snapped her out of her erotic fantasies, "But I might have a position for you that thousands of women would vie for. But it's a tricky position and you'd have to grab it right away. I'm sure the position will be gone soon. It would be a great opportunity and it's a once in a lifetime one," Luna fluted and sighed deeply.

All of a sudden, Stell's alarm bells went off. A big chance? An opportunity for her? And on top of that, a job that many other women would love to have? What could it possibly be about? Apparently she liked her. Because why else would Luna offer her a job when neither of them had really talked about her resume or anything yet?

"What kind of a job are we talking about?" asked Stell, tugging uneasily at her suit.

"It's an assistant position. We need an assistant for our senior manager Malaika. She has one by now, however she is so completely overloaded with her duties that Malaika has asked us to hire someone else. And that's where you come in," Luna smiled and batted her eyelashes, looking at Stell with a face like sugar.

"I'm not sure..."

"Stell, let's get real here! Working for our company is your dream, isn't it?"

"Yes, it is, but..."

"Then no but, but let's go! You have a unique chance here to become Malaika's new assistant. She is only one step below our CEO. You'll be working for the best of the best, so to speak. And just like that. I'm offering you this position. Grab it before it's too late!" Luna looked like she was giving a speech. It was solemn. Stell almost had to laugh.

"Uh-huh, okay. I see. Yes, that sounds exciting..." she stammered.

But that statement was enough for Luna and she grabbed the phone in a flash. A few seconds later, Stell was back in the elevator and headed back down a few floors to get into the conversation ring with the junior assistant, soon to be senior assistant, Serena. She was a stunning beauty. Stell was amazed at how skinny she was. Her stomach literally bulged inward and her hip bones stood out clearly. Stell scanned her spindly legs and swallowed. She looked so fragile, like a glass doll. Serena wore tight leather pants that seemed like a second skin. She also wore a pink tank top that stretched over her expansive round breasts. After looking Serena up and down again, she knew for a fact that those bust lines weren't real. If you had so little body fat, then you couldn't show off breasts like that. There was no way. I wonder what they would feel like. Were they firm or more soft and malleable? Her mind wandered once again and she blushed a little. Serena took an instant liking to her. The latter laughed briefly, tossing back her long fawn hair, which spread like a long shiny cape down her elfin back. Serena's fingers and toenails were painted a soft pink, glowing with every movement. Her high-heeled shoes made her look even taller and more elegant. Almost intimidating. She was at least five foot eight. Serena looked sexy, half-naked and classy all at the same time. Stell was mesmerised by her beauty.

"Hello, I'm Serena. But I'm sure you already know that. I was once one of the models myself. But then I wanted to get out of the limelight and work behind the scenes instead," she introduced herself in her bell-bright voice, tugging at her top.

"You must be Stell. I'm glad to meet you. If you want, I'll show you around," Serena spoke through her ever-white teeth.

"That would be great, thank you Serena. You look amazing," Stell said and she got hot and cold at the same time looking at Serena.

"I've just been promoted, so Malaika is desperate for a replacement. Of course, the work days are long. Long as hell. Sometimes you're just working and sleeping in the office because it wouldn't be worth it to go home. I've often worked till five in the morning, then slept in the office for two hours and then it was back to work. But that's normal. If you want to get high, you have to do something for it. My life as a model was even more exhausting, I can promise you that Stell," Serena sighed to her. Her lips were so full and seemed so velvety soft. Stell wanted to kiss her so badly, right here, right now.

"Stell, are you even listening to me?" asked Serena, snapping her out of her thoughts.

"Yeah, sure thing. The work days are long and you've slept in the office before," Stell repeated monotonously and took a deep breath.

"Exactly. If you manage to stick it out here, all doors and gates will be open to you. If you have talent and flair, you can make it pretty far pretty fast..." Serena said, her eyes looking slightly misty.

They walked together criss-cross through the large building. Stell was introduced to all the people and her feet were soon burning. She had never been taken so long at a job interview. When the interview with Serena was over, she whispered briefly in her ear, "I think we'll meet again soon. And I'm sure this will be sooner than you think Stell. You are so hot..."

Stell's heart was pounding in her throat. Her lips and mouth were dry as dust. She was so exhausted and aroused at the same time that she was about to lie down on the cream-colored sofa in the reception room so she could close her eyes for a brief moment, when she heard the next pair of high heels and rolled her eyes. Then she turned to see the next rank slender creature striding towards her. Her long silver blonde hair fell down her back in long waves. It turned out to be her new boss, Malaika.

Stell was once again so captivated by the elegance, which radiated this wonderful woman. Malaika wore a tight leather skirt, which was so short that you actually had to put on no skirt. A sheer pale pink blouse let Stell catch a glimpse of a beautiful white lace bra and again she chewed her lower lip in embarrassment. To go with it, her delicate white painted feet were in black strappy sandals. In addition, her skin was perfectly tanned and basically the young woman was wearing so much bare skin on display that this outfit really ought to be forbidden. Never would she dare to go to work like that. Malaika stopped a few inches in front of her, eyed her from head to toe, walked around her once and then stopped very close to her nose. She was taller than Stell and Stell's eyes stared at her cleavage.

"What brings you to us, Stell?" fluted Malaika's bell-bright voice.

"I had a job interview. I was invited to come here. I think I fit in well here," she huffed, looking up somewhat innocently. The two's eyes met and lightning bolts literally twitched between them.

"Is that what you think? You think you're up to the work here? You think you're up to us?" she asked Malaika, stroking her shoulder with her long manicured fingers. A comforting shiver came over her and for seconds she closed her eyes.

"You like that?" she asked Stell, then continued stroking her back down to her bottom.

"Yes, very much so..." breathed Stell.

"I'm the boss here," Malaika whispered in Stell's ear, then nibbled. "Would you like to come to my office? We could continue our conversation there. After all, I need to get to know you as well and know about your skills. If you do well, there should be nothing in the way of hiring you," Malaika stroked Stell's lips with her finger and then took her hand.

Stell walked hesitantly behind Malaika, her heart pounding in her throat. She was nervous. Excited and aroused at the same time. All the feelings and impressions were pouring down on her. Her office was behind a wide white wooden door at the end of the hall. The office was very sterilely furnished with a wide white sofa, an L-shaped desk on which stood an unfolded laptop and some file baskets.

Malaika closed the door behind her and pressed her directly against the wall. Although she was so petite, there was tremendous strength behind her grip. Malaika took it all in, unbuttoning Stell's blazer along with her blouse and taking her breasts in her hands. She kneaded them vigorously, pushing her tongue down her throat as she did so. Not at all timid, but stormy and demanding. Stell was literally left breathless, but she too wanted to explore Malaika. Thank God she was wearing such a skimpy skirt. In no time at all Stell had pushed the skirt up, pushed the little piece of cloth, which was called a thong, to the side and already she was running her fingers along Malaika's vulva. She was completely shaved and immediately flinched at any careful touch from her. This pleased Stell and since this was part of the interview, she already wanted to leave a good impression.

Stell ran her fingers between Malaika's slightly spread legs and let first one and then a second finger slide into her vagina. She was wet and warm. Then she stretched Malaika and began to move her fingers inside her. In and out. Faster and faster and faster.

"How wet you are..." gasped Stell, quickening her rhythm. Stell heard Malaika moan loudly and she pressed her lower body towards her fingers.

"Do it faster for me! Try a little harder," Malaika pressed out under her quivering voice and Stell did as she was told.

She let another finger slide into her and pressed her clit with her thumb. This was too much for Malaika and she came with a suppressed cry and trembled all over. She looked at Stell with glowing big eyes and pressed a kiss on her lips.

"I would like to play with you Stell a little more before I make my decision. But I would like to get another opinion on board...", Malaika spoke and directed her gaze to the door.

This opened silently and Stell saw Luna and Serena float in. They were wearing - nothing. Her mouth stayed open and her tongue was dry as dust. Stell's breath rose and fell at a rate and she felt like she was about to pass out. Stell was surrounded by the most beautiful women in the world. Serena and Luna came up to her, took her in their midst and rubbed their hot bodies against Stell. The latter felt their nipples on her skin. Serena stood behind her, sliding her fingers over her belly, stripping off her pants, and Luna helped Serena from the front. In seconds, Stell was stark naked as well. Serena slid her fingers down to her pussy from behind and rubbed it vigorously. Stell sighed loudly and Luna took her nipples into her mouth, sucking and sucking hard on them.

"She's so hot... the perfect toy for us," Serena murmured, sliding three fingers into Stell at once. She spread her labia wide and Luna's tongue disappeared into her wet vulva as well.

"Oh my god, please don't..." she pleaded aloud, her legs going soft. She braced herself against them, pressing Luna's head against her vagina, wanting to fuck her mouth.

Then she heard Malaika coming towards her. She was holding some sextoys in her hand. Stell widened her eyes and tensed up.

"We like to play erotic games. Play with us Stell! " Malaika pulled Stell to her on the couch with the sex toys and then put the dildo in her mouth in front of her. She licked and sucked on it and I looked at her with my mouth open. Then she grabbed a couple of silver love balls and held them out to me.

"Go on, lick it. Show me how good your tongue is," Malaika asked her and she took the cool round silver balls with slightly trembling fingers. Then she half opened her mouth and slid both balls into my mouth. The cool silver immediately became warm and wet.

"Sit in front of me and spread your legs as wide as you can. Like me...", Malaika asked her and sat in front of her.

Stell could see her beautiful shaved vagina and moaned. Luna and Serena also joined her on the couch and started playing with each other. They positioned themselves in the sixty-nine position and licked each other. Stell was distracted for a moment, but Malaika shook her head.

"Just concentrate on me now Stell," then Malaika licked over the dildo again and slowly pushed it very deep into Stell's vulva. This filled her completely and she gasped.

"Oh no, Malaika, I can't go on," Stell's voice trembled.

"We haven't even started yet. Try a little harder, Stell. Come on now, I want to feel something too. Put the balls in me," Malaika whispered and guided her hand to her already wet pussy.

Stell stretched her labia apart and then pushed her first one and then the second love ball deep inside. At the end was a ribbon and then she pulled again and again. Malaika put her head in the neck and she also moved the dildo rhythmically in Stell's pussy.

"Come on Stell, faster... Come on! ", she shouted and opened her legs even wider.

Together they worked each other's wet pussies and Malaika pressed Stell again and again against the dildo, which disappeared deeper and deeper inside her.

"Stell, I want to do something else to you... Come on, give me the dildo too, please," Malaika moaned and then turned around provocatively so that Malaika's sugary sweet ass was sticking out towards her.

"What do you want from me?" asked Stell, kissing her bottom.

"I want to feel the dildo in my ass. Deeply. I need it badly because you make me so hot," Malaika moaned, looking heated.

"Don't you have a strap-on?" asked Stell, looking into her astonished eyes.

"Sure, wait," Serena gasped, looking up from Luna's wet pussy and quickly running to the drawer of Malaika's desk. She pulled out a large black dildo to strap on. Stell's eyes gazed greedily at it.

Quickly she ran to Stell with it, then sucked briefly over the dildo and made herself over Luna again. Then Stell strapped on the strap-on and positioned herself behind Malaika. Greedy as a lion, she gazed at her prey. Adrenaline shot into her blood.

"You have terrific ideas. That's the kind of employee I like Stell," Malaika begged, sticking her ass out at her again.

Then Stell took her ass in his hands and licked Malaika over the anus. She moaned and clawed herself into the sofa. Stell moistened the dildo again and then carefully slid it into her tight anus. Malaika gasped loudly, leaned on her hands and Stell grasped her hips. Then she pushed first carefully and a short time later harder and harder.

"Fuck Stell, you're amazing. Please try really hard, don't let me down!" cried Malaika, throwing her long silver blonde hair back and biting her lips.

Stell pulled her towards him by her hair, moving her hips faster and faster as he did so, grabbing her breasts and taking all of her. Stell wanted Malaika and the job. She wanted it all at any cost. Again and again the dildo slid into her anus and then Stell reached for the string on the love ball and pulled it out of her vulva with a jerk.

"Ah, damn you bitch!" cried Malaika, shuddering all over her body.

Stell pulled the dildo out of her anus, threw Malaika impetuously onto her back, lay over her and then with another jerk pushed the dildo back into her wet pussy.

"Get it for me Stell, fuck me! Please..." she gasped, her eyes shining.

Then suddenly she felt two tongues behind her. Luna and Serena knelt behind her ass, pulled her buttocks apart and sank their tongues into her anus. Quickly their fingers disappeared into her tight hole and she quivered with lust and passion. Stell grasped Malaika's legs, pulled her close, and then thrust hard and relentlessly again and again. Malaika quivered, reared up under her and cried out her name again and again as a breathtaking orgasm overcame her.

Completely detached, Stell lay down next to Malaika, her eyes closed. She heard her breathing rapidly and her chest rising and falling quickly. Luna and Serena joined Stell and her boss on the sofa and a film of sweat appeared on their bodies.

"I'm very impressed with you Stell. You got the job. I've never had such a terrific interview. Welcome to Agent Provocateur!", Malaika sighed, pulled Stell close once more and pressed a passionate kiss to her lips.

Hard physical work just paid off again and again....

In Übersehn 9
51570 Windeck

13-digit KDP-ISBN: 9798369953044

Cover design by: LUGO media
www.lugo-media.com

www.ingramcontent.com/pod-product-compliance
Lightning Source LLC
La Vergne TN
LVHW041238150826
845673LV00008B/2420

9798369953044